Diary of an Odd Enderman

Book 1

An Unofficial Minecraft Series

By Mr. Crafty

Contents

Contents

Day 1

I am Enderman. That's what everybody calls me. I'm not always okay with my looks, but I guess it's alright if I talk about it in my diary, right?! I have long legs, lanky arms, all black, and purple glowing eyes. In a way, I feel like I look intimidating enough to keep creatures away from me. I don't really feel like talking to them anyway.

It's not easy to live in a world as dark and cold as my home, but it is my home. It's where I feel safe to relax and just be me. I'm not an angry being, but I do know how to defend myself if it's needed. They teach us that here.

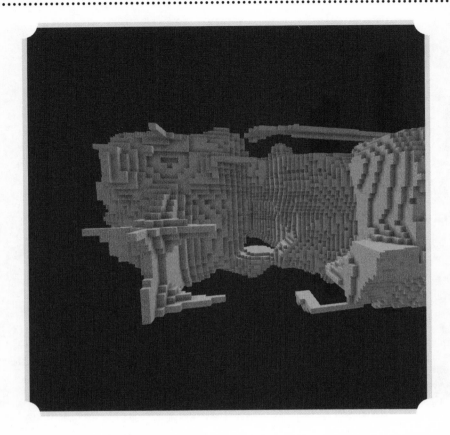

My world is dark. Looking all around my comforting world, I see islands. Floating islands. I see these islands raised above an endless sea of complete darkness. I often wonder why it's so dreary here. When I do that, I think about what other worlds might look like. I've heard stories of other endermen traveling to colorful worlds. They think they can experience some sort of happiness beyond what we have here. They are wrong.

All they saw were these human creatures attacking animals for food and taking over beautiful nature by building and building some more. They were greedy. I get it. Everybody needs to eat. I just can't understand why they take over so much land with their buildings. It takes away from its natural green beauty. They are so lucky to have colors to look at every day, and they don't even know it. The other endermen that I live with don't even seem to care about the creatures they saw there or the land they live on. They just want to steal what they have, if they even had anything to take in the first place. Why do I feel so different from my people? Is there something wrong with me or is it all of them?

The stories that the older endermen share often make me wonder if I should take a journey into other colorful worlds in the future. Should I only believe it if I see it with my own glowing eyes? I'm curious. The others bring back so much from that other world, so is there anything left to see? I do have my powers and I'm confident that I can find what I'm looking for. I can protect myself with my intimidating looks! Oh diary, what should I do?

Day 2

I am glad I decided to start my own diary. I'm writing for the second day in a row and I already feel like you're listening to me. You understand my feelings and this is my safe place to let out all of my emotions. I can't do that around the others. I know that I am different from them. Today is the same type of day that yesterday was. It's still very dark and cold here. My world will always be that way. I wish it were colorful, with bright green trees and grass as the others describe when they come back from the other land.

I am one of the younger endermen in my group. I often wonder why the elders seem so cruel. All they want is to steal things from the human creatures! When they were younger, did they question the meaning of life at all? Their imagination and creative mind must have vanished at some point. Didn't they ever want to do something good for the world? I really have no idea. I've spent most nights wondering if I can reach out to one of them to ask why we live this way and ask if there is something wrong with me for thinking differently.

Courage is hard for me when I think about how that conversation would go. So, for now, I'm going to write to you and I'm going to plan my journey. Of course, I'm terrified! The fear of the unknown is a strong feeling. I'm ready to find out if I can overcome the fear of a new adventure and a new world. I want to see what this is all about. I promise that I will write down everything that happens. Oh wow, now I'm starting to get really excited! Okay, I'm going to go to bed now. Tomorrow will be a new day and I shall begin my plans for my first ever trip through the portal! Woohoo!!

Day 3

O kay, so let's get this plan started. The smart thing to do would be to travel at night. Hopefully, the other creatures are sleeping at that time. I can't stand the thought of creatures being all around me. You know I've never been around any creatures other than my own, right? Every day when we gather after lunch, all the endermen listen to stories together. We all sit in a circle with the storyteller right in the middle, and I listen carefully to every word. I remember my favorite stories that have been told by the elders. When the elder shares the "Tales of Ninjas," I can't look away from him as he explains what he encountered in the other world. He has come across a creature that can move fast as lightning, just like we do! There is a difference though. The ninja defends the land from enemies with his swift moves. We, as endermen, tend to be known as one of those enemies. After I hear the ninja stories, I always go back to my favorite tower in my world and pretend that I am a ninja defeating one enemy at a time! I don't think any of the others have witnessed me doing this. At least, I hope not!

Alright, so I will start my journey tomorrow night. I think I just walk into the portal and it takes me there. If I end up somewhere different than the beautiful world the others have described, then I'll just go back through the portal, right? Oh, I guess I really don't know what I'm doing. Oh well, I have to do this. So, I'll walk into the portal at night and... Wait, what's it going to feel like when I go into this portal?

Do I dissolve into a million pieces and float in the air? Maybe I'm thinking too much.

When I get to the nature-filled world, I want to look around and explore. I can't let anyone see me! That's very important! I only know what the other endermen tell me about the other creatures. I have to be sneaky, clever and very quiet about this. I can do it! I know I can if I put my mind to it. I'll give myself one hour to discover my surroundings. If I need more time than that and everything seems to be going okay, then I'll stay longer. I guess I just want to tell myself to try to stay there for a whole hour the first night, even if I am a little scared. Setting goals is a good thing, right?

Being all alone there makes me nervous as well. I'll never discover anything new if I don't push myself to do things that I am scared to do. I really want to do this, so it's a plan. Please portal, don't make me feel like I am a bunch of cocoa beans being thrown into a pot of rabbit stew! Ha! Yes, my imagination is something out of this world! Let's do this! Tomorrow night!!!!

Day 4

Ahhh, diary, I did it! I made it to the other world! Okay, okay, let me explain everything! First of all, the portal did not make me feel like tiny pieces of cocoa beans floating around. It actually made me feel like I was spinning in a whirlwind instead. It was fun! My body felt like it was flying with the wind in every direction! What a ride!

Anyways, let me start from the beginning. Last night before I left, I was so nervous, but that wasn't going to stop me. No way! I had to be sneaky to make sure I wasn't caught by the others. Oh boy, was it scary! I'm pretty quiet though. Wait one second, I'll be right back. I'm suddenly craving a baked potato. Luckily, I packed myself a lunch!

Okay, I'm back. That was delicious. I'm chewing up my last bite right now. Where was I? Oh, the portal! That was the perfect time for me to finally practice the ninja moves I learned from the elders' stories! I crept around to the entrance of the portal, without any of the others noticing me! Hmm, being a ninja when I grow up might be a good idea. I was so nervous, but nobody was watching. The adults talk to each other a lot. Mostly they have boring conversations and brag about how much they can steal and attack others. I had ninja moves to do, I had no time to listen to that nonsense. I spoke very calmly to the portal, as if it could really hear me. I said, "Now portal, I do not want to turn into chopped up food." It must have listened to me because soon I felt I had the courage to jump in. Actually, I swear it said something back to me. What am I saying? That's impossible!

I stood in front of the portal and collected my thoughts for a second or two. Bending my long legs (probably looking extremely awkward), I jumped in. Whoosh! Wind was tunneling around my body with the force of a tornado. Mayday! Ninja in distress!!! I was right smack in the middle of a disaster, or so I thought. I started to spin in circles at a crazy speed. Okay, at least I wasn't being chopped up into pieces, right? Bam! Moments later, I arrived in one piece at my destination. I kind of liked that spinning feeling. It's a fun ride, besides being a little dizzy afterwards.

I was hesitant at first. I was in a completely unknown place. I took my first step onto this weird green, furry floor. I started swaying to the right and fell to the ground, like a person would do after spinning around with their head on a long stick. That's exactly what it reminded me of! All the young endermen like to play this game where we have a tall stick, stuck in the ground. Then we place our block head at the top of the stick. While holding the stick right underneath our head, we spin really fast in a thousand circles. The final step is to try to walk around to see if we can walk straight! Hahaha!

Anyways, I stepped out of the portal and… Plop! My body went down like a wet and wiggly fish. Wow, that probably looked weird. After the dizziness started to fade, I got up slowly. Thank goodness nobody saw that! Whew!

I started to walk on this green pointy stuff. I've learned from the others that they call it grass. So, this is what grass looks and feels like! I told myself to explore this new world for at least an hour. Yeah, that didn't happen. I took about ten steps towards a light I saw in the distance, and then out of nowhere I heard this insane noise to the left of me.

It freaked me out, so I quickly jumped back into the portal's spinning whirlwind to go back home. Well, that was a start for me. I think tomorrow night I'll bring you along with me so I can write down all the details as I explore. I would hate to forget anything I experienced, even though I think that's probably impossible! I need to find a pack around here to put you in, so I can keep you safe as well. I can't wait until tomorrow!

Day 5

It isn't technically nighttime right now. Living in this world that's always dark, you get used to figuring out when it's morning and evening. What we see outside is always the same. Boring wouldn't even be the correct word to describe it. When it comes time for me to jump in that awesome ride in the portal, I'm bringing you along with me safe and sound, in the pack I found!

Oh, I made a rhyme in that sentence! Hehe! Sound and found!! Oh my goodness, that reminds me of the time that an enderman came back from the world beyond with this book. In the book, there were pages of something the villagers call a "poem." It was a beautiful book to read. The villager that wrote the rhyming poems wrote that way to describe his experiences. I want to try that someday! I'm sure I can make lovely poems about my adventures!

If I have time to write when I get there, I will. If not, don't worry! I'll write as soon as I have a chance because I need to remember everything about my adventure!

I'll make sure to write down every detail, and maybe someday I can write a book like the villagers do! Time to go now, diary!

Whoa! Alright, I'm in the world with the pointy grass everywhere. Looks like the same place as last night. I think I can get used to the crazy portal ride. All the fear I had the first time has completely vanished! Turning into chopped up beans or rabbit stew will not happen to my limber body. I'm taking a note of that right now. This is good. This is very good. I still get very dizzy and have a hard time walking straight. Noted. Just take it easy when you step out onto the ground.

I'm going to put you in my pack now so that I can go explore.

I'm back home now. Since I have time to write now, I'll tell you everything that happened on the other side. After I stepped out of the portal, I kept extremely quiet. My goal was to be as sneaky as possible. Also, I needed to put my strong ninja face on, and face my fears. I told myself to not run away from scary or unknown noises, but I still needed to avoid creatures at all costs. If I came across anything that spooked me, I had the advantage of being sneaky and quick! If I heard one creepy noise that really freaked me out, then I told my brain that I should just close my eyes and hiss until everything is quiet again. I felt like I could be brave and handle any situation that I came across.

I saw a lot tonight! You would never believe what it felt like to see trees for the first time! I've heard the others describe them before, so I knew exactly what I was looking at, but they never told me how truly amazing they are to gaze upon! The trees grew so high up in the sky, that it was hard to see where the treetops ended. There was a light again in the distance. I knew that was probably where the villagers lived. At least, that's what I thought. To do good things for the world, I needed to get there. I was on a mission to find out if any human needed help, or even any creature! I wondered how I was going to know if they even needed help in the first place? I would have to make sure that they were asleep or not home when I approached the village.

I stood there motionless, staring at the far distant light, and continued to look up towards the lovely trees in a complete daze. The smell in the air was so sweet. Flowers. I've decided that flowers are nice. All of their vivid colors were noticeable even in the dark night. Oh, and the moon! The moon was like a bright white spotlight shining on the grass and the trees and the flowers. It was amazing!

While I was taking in the scenery, I heard that weird noise again. I said to myself, "Be strong Enderman. Be brave!" My fingers are trembling slightly, so I'm sorry if my handwriting is not so good right now. I just can't stop thinking about how exciting it was! Okay, so I looked around. I didn't see anything. I thought for a while and then I came up with a clever idea! I have the ability to teleport. If I teleported closer to the light, I'd be there in a flash, so that is what I did.

I didn't get too close, but I have good vision, so I could see everything. There were these enormous buildings and little houses. It looked like a tornado had been through there! Huge blocks piling on top of each other, holes in structures that look like there should be something there. I bet the other endermen stole those pieces! I saw a garden where food should be. There was nothing there. Just brown dirt and water spilling out of the side. So much was missing from that place. There's no way that half of a building would look perfect and the other half would just look horrible. Is that on purpose?

This is where it gets scary. I saw something else. Right behind a little patch of sweet-smelling flowers, a green figure started to walk towards me. It looked so creepy and did not say a single word to me. I'm still really upset about what happened next. The weird green thing got close enough to look directly into my purple eyes. I don't know what happened or how it happened, but I feel terrible about it! It felt like I blacked out for a moment. Once he looked at my eyes, my body started shaking and it's like I moved without telling my brain to do so! I started to attack this creature!! I could not control what I was doing at all!

Thank goodness the creature was able to escape! He went straight into what I think is known as a lake. My family told me that a lake is made of liquid, which means you can go right through it, and it has little ripples and shines the moonlight back up at you. This creeper knew that because I'm an enderman I cannot be in water. It destroys me. On the bright side, at least he's okay. It seems like he has come across an enderman before, and that's how he knew to jump into the lake.

With my heart pounding, I quickly returned to my world. After feeling myself go into attack mode, and start acting like a bully I just wanted to get home. I can't let any creature look directly into my eyes. That's when it all happened!! I just can't be here! I don't want to hurt anything, no matter what! I don't even know if that green creepy thing was trying to harm me in the first place! I'm so scared now. I have to find a way to change this about me. I need to be able to control myself around other creatures! Ninjas learn control, so I know that I can too!

Tomorrow evening is a new night and will be a new adventure. Time to gather my notes and come up with a genius plan to get a little closer to the houses I saw. Also, I will work on maintaining control of my actions if a creature happens to lock eyes with me. Since there wasn't any food growing in the garden, I'm going to bring a chest of food and leave it outside one of the houses!

Day 6

Hi diary! Today is a new day and I am gaining more and more courage to explore the world! While looking for food items for the villagers, I found lots of yummy things to fill their bellies! Sneaking around my world comes easier every day. With my swift ninja moves, none of the others have spotted me. There are plenty of empty and lonely chests around that I can fill with deliciousness! I have gathered apples, cookies, cooked chicken, bread, and for a little extra fun, I added melon and wheat seeds. This is a great start!

The empty chest is now filled and ready to go to its destination. The chest will survive through the portal. I know how this portal works now, and I'm not afraid at all, since I tackled that like a pro! Of course, the most important thing to bring along is you, diary! So, into my pack you go and hold on tight! We are about to walk into this fun ride once again!

We are here! Back into the stunning, beautiful world that I love to see. It seems to be the perfect time to write for a moment. I still get the same dizzy feeling when I come here. I stand outside of the portal, and I give myself a little bit of time to collect my brain and feel better. I look around for a moment to appreciate all of the wonders I see and smell right before me. Every time I have gone through the portal, nobody was around. The chest is with me and I shall teleport to the village lights. I remind myself, "Do not get frightened of sounds or movements!" I will write more very soon!

Oh man!! Okay, I'm back at home now and I'm trying to collect my thoughts to tell you what happened in the world beyond! Where do I start?! As soon as I put my diary back into my pack, I teleported quickly to the village. The lights that I saw there helped to show me the way! As I stood there quietly, I witnessed one of my fellow endermen doing exactly what I'm not ever going to do! Stealing!! He was undoing everything I wanted to do to help these poor villagers! Oh well, I guess whatever one of my own steals, I'll just bring back to its rightful owner. Hehe!

He seemed aggressive and was right next to a villager! I saw a villager!! That was the first time I have actually seen one! Whoa! One villager was building a statue and it looked like the enderman was trying to steal from it. I wish the other endermen didn't act so vicious. The villager threw a bucket of water at him. I couldn't help but to chuckle, very quietly, because this was really funny. Water, in any form, will hurt us. Rain is something we all need to stay away from. But watching one of my own have water thrown at him serves him right! We should never steal from others!

Well, that was a sticky situation! After that fun-filled moment, I crept around slowly and looked in every direction. I was ready to make my move. Feeling anxious, I gathered my thoughts. Most of the villagers were either asleep or not home. There was one house that looked rather beat up in my opinion, with empty gardens that should be filled with colorful crops. This is the house I wanted to give the chest of food to.

There I went, walking as slowly as a turtle, taking every step with care. The wind was howling as it swirled around my lanky body. Taking a deep breath of fresh air, I made my move. Placing the chest down very gently, I looked around to see if anyone was watching. As I stood there, the howling of the wind comforted me. I did it! The chest was there, right where I wanted it to be!

Then, all of a sudden, I saw movement. The wind was getting louder, making my ears ring with its howling. Suddenly, I didn't feel as comfortable anymore. What was that? What was that creature that was peeking at me from behind that tall tree? I took a minute to reflect on the stories from the elders and then I finally knew what it was! I've learned a lot about the world beyond my home, after all. It was a wolf! This white and gray dog has been watching me explore this world. It wasn't the wind howling, it was him! I had to get out of there. I have not yet taught myself how to control my attack mode. I can't harm anything! I can't live with that thought!

Thankfully, I made it back safe and sound! That whole night was more frightening to me than water! Tomorrow, I need to practice. The best kind of practice that I can think of is trying to think like a ninja. Control. I can practice control on a dirt block! Yeah, there are a lot of dirt blocks here because, you know, we steal them!

Day 7

My morning has been amazing so far! I decided to teach myself how to control my anger when something locks eyes with me! I need to master this!! It's important to me to try to change the way others see us. The other creatures think we are thieves and villains, but I want to show them that we can be friendly too! I can make a difference, right? If not, at least I can try!

I was as fast as a ninja and moved like the wind! I went to a place in my ugly world where I could be alone and showed that dirt block that I was there to fight! Of course, that was on purpose. I destroyed half of it, then I told myself deep within to stop! Stop hurting that innocent dirt block! I asked myself, "Enderman, how would you feel if that dirt block loses its life?!" At first, it was very hard to stop attacking. Once my brain went into attack mode, it was tricky to get myself out of that zone. I did this over and over again until the night started to creep in. I wanted so badly to be able to do good, and with a strong heart, and a little hard work, I was able to make a lot of progress in controlling my anger!

Now, when I think about the wolf, it scares me. Maybe, just maybe, he is like me. He might be kind-hearted, and I should not judge him because I've heard scary things about wolves. It's hard to not think of him that way, but I can't let this ruin the good things I want to do. I'm going back. If the chest is gone from that doorstep, I'll know that I accomplished what I set out to do.! I will bring you along, you awesome companion of mine! I wonder what it would be like if you could talk back to me. I kind of wish you could! Me doing all the talking makes me feel like I talk too much!

Who am I kidding?!? Of course, I talk a lot! I am one odd enderman!

I have a moment to write. I am in the other world. This place gets to me every time. Chickens are speaking with a "cluck, cluck" as they roam around innocently. I think they're rather cute! Rolling green hills create a peaceful environment and the flowers, oh the flowers. I'm going to sniff this bright red one. Ah, it smells magical!

Now it is time to use my advanced speed to reach the lovely houses surrounded by clear streams, pointy, yet soft grass, and towering trees. Yes, I will stay away from the rushing streams, but they are rather peaceful to gaze upon. I will fill you in with my adventures for the night very soon!

Hello again, diary. I'm back home again, ready to fill you with all the things that happened to me in the other world. When I got to the village, there were broken-down houses, roaming animals, and broken fences. I'm guessing the animals were supposed to be inside the fences, not running around everywhere. The chest of food was missing. Okay, this could mean two things here: Either my mission was completed and the villager got a lucky surprise when he woke up or something horrible happened, and my own kind felt greedy deep down, and stole it back!

I went to look through a glass window to see if I could get a better view of the inside. There it was! Yes! I did it! The chest was opened ever so slightly. The apple was set into a black bowl on top of the kitchen counter. My first mission was a success and this guy had no idea who left him the chest in the first place. I'm afraid if he does find out or catches me around his village, he might try to defend himself and attack me. I'm still learning how to control my anger, so I do not know what would happen if I came in contact with a villager!

The animals weren't getting too close to me at that time. There were chickens, and cows, and what I believe are called pigs. What funny creatures they are. They make a snorting sound and I was trying with all my might to only laugh in my head. Nobody wants to hear my laugh. My laugh sounds very similar to the pig's snort. The other endermen raise their eyebrows at me every time I laugh too hard.

I wish I had a way to learn what else I can do to help others, without risking my amusing life. If I go there during the day to witness people working or to act like a secret agent spying on their conversations, I might learn how I can secretly help. That's too risky for me. You know what? I saw where the garden should be and I think I've realized why the villager had not yet planted the melon and wheat seeds I gave him. Maybe he doesn't have the proper tools. We have plenty of tools back here at home. But if I continue to help, will my family just keep stealing things? I'm rather smart and very creative. I can figure this out.

Anyways, since I tend to get off track... There I was, peeking in the villager's window with the animals walking all around me. I turned to leave and, in the distance, behind that same tall tree, the wolf was staring straight into my purple eyes. Was it the same wolf that had been spying on me? I was hesitant, but I continued to stand tall, motionless. Diary, he started to creep slowly towards me! I took a deep breath. Nothing happened, so I took another deep breath! Why was he looking at me with those confused puppy eyes?

Something amazing happened! You will never believe this! As I was getting ready to make my sprint towards the portal, the wolf spoke to me! He asked me, through the rushing wind, to please not run away. Shocked, I stood there for a moment wondering if I should trust him. Should I even trust myself? Am I able to look in his eyes and be kind to him at the same time? I decided to listen to him. It was a risk, but I wanted to believe that he was just like me. I know it's not fair to judge another creature based on his intimidating looks or based on the actions of others of his kind.

Right this moment, I am sitting under a moonlit sky and far away from the village. The wolf is relaxing right next to me. I have not attacked him, and he did not attack me. This is awesome! I was able to control my thoughts of attacking him and it worked! I know I still need to be careful because this is all new to me.

His name is River and he immediately explained his curiosity about me! River was the one who was ever so quietly watching me. He couldn't understand why I was sneaking around the village and why I placed the chest of food at the door. River has never seen an enderman act this way. I get it. I'm different and I've always known that. He wants to help me because he too wants to have adventures and new experiences.

This is exactly what I need. Actually, it's exactly what River needs too. He's had a hard life and, somehow, we seem to understand each other. So, this is what a friendship feels like! River and I had a long and thoughtful talk. He is going to gather information for me during the day, since he knows I can't be around when everyone's awake. Tomorrow, we are going to meet here, on top of this grassy hill underneath the tree where we first met. Oh, by the way, River says "Hi!" I'd better be getting home now.

Day 8

L ast night, I had a dream in which wonderful trees and flowers were sprouting from the floating islands of my dark world. Nature was spreading and growing everywhere in beautiful colors! When I woke up, I realized that I've already done a lot to make the world a better place. I feel proud. Proud that I have faced my fears of the unknown, and proud to now call River my friend. I have never once thought that this could be a reality for me. While I venture out on missions to help others, I'm filled with overwhelming joy. I guess when you embark on a journey, anything can happen. Whether it's a good situation or a bad one, I have to take in each situation carefully as I wander further into my dream of doing good.

I have decided to bring handy tools along for this villager to help him plant his garden, so that it has a chance to become the tasty food that he deserves. Give me a few minutes to sneak around my home. I know there are tools here that we don't even use. Most likely, these tools have been selfishly stolen from the villagers to begin with. I must stop that horrid trend. That is the ultimate plan, but for now, I have to take things one step at a time.

Here we go! I found this shiny iron hoe behind one of the towering structures that rise above our land. It was just lying there, as if the hoe were begging me to pick it up and give it to someone in need. Okay, shiny iron hoe, your wish is my command! Into my pack you go! Time to head out, diary. I'll let you know how it went after I get back!

It's me again, diary. So, here is what happened tonight on my adventure. The portal spinning ride never gets old. Hehe! I arrived on the other side with the garden tool. I always take a brief look around to take in my surroundings. I was in the clear to start traveling towards the tree to meet with River. I saw him. His fluffy fur coat and intimidating eyes glaring at me as if he wanted to eat me for dinner. It's okay, I told myself. That's River, my new friend.

River told me that he explored the village area during the day to gain a better idea of what has happened to their buildings and to sit back and observe the villagers. The people there work all day long, sweating but never giving up. Their survival instincts are fascinating. I wish I could watch them as they try to thrive within their environment. Maybe one day I will be brave enough to come during the day. For now, my sidekick friend is willing to help me and help others.

River and I made our way towards the village. I saw the light on, reminding me of the very scary first trip I made there all on my own. Oh man! My clumsy nature and fear of the unknown show so clearly. It makes it worse when someone sees this side of me. I fell face first into the pointy grass when something flew, whooshing right by my head!! River would not stop laughing. It was more of a howl than a laugh. I needed a minute. I felt a snorting laugh coming from my belly and I was about to explode with heavy, joyful laughter. Once my laughter erupted, I heard it echoing all around me, loud as the Ender Dragon!

I found out that the creepy flying creature was a bat. A bat? I don't quite know what a bat is, but that seems like such a small word for something that looked so vicious and can fly!! A bat? I don't understand, but I guess it's a black mouse type creature with vampire wings. That's how River explained it. Haha! Sounds like a spooky story being told in the dark around a firepit! Well, even though I was scared at first, that was thrilling! I told River the show is over now. You can stop laughing! Haha!

We placed the iron hoe in front of the wooden door to the house. I went very slowly, like a turtle, and it seemed like I held my breath each time I made a move. Actually, I don't even know what a turtle looks like. The elders have shared stories, saying that it's a creature that has a hard shell and walks extremely slowly. Haha! They don't sound as scary as a bat. Now I kind of want to meet a turtle!

We left the village to go back to our meeting spot on the grassy hill. Tomorrow, River and I have decided to have more adventures and he is going to show me around. I haven't seen much of this world. What I have seen is more amazing than I ever imagined, but River tells me there is even more to this world that will blow my mind!

Day 9

Wow, diary! Last night, River showed me so many amazing new things about his world! It's changed the way I look at life. Reflecting on what I witnessed, I decided to write this diary entry as a poem. It's my turn to try out what I've seen in the books from the villagers! I do like rhyming. For example: In my journal, I hope to write about a turtle. What is a bat, but a flying rat? Ninjas are fast, as I sit here still an outcast. Ha! See!! Oh, this will be fun!

Being creative with my words will be a relaxing way for me to share my experiences. As I sit back home by a boring old rock, thoughts are starting to come to me and now I shall tell you what I have seen. Let's give this poem thing a shot! Here is how I saw the world beyond last night with my friend River at my side.

A bright circle from above is shining down,
Leading its light to reflect from the ground.
The moon dances on the rushing water,

And the movement it creates makes
not a single sound.
Peaceful music not made with
instruments, But with pure nature itself:
Animals, whooshing, breathing in
the air, Or Books resting easy on a shelf.

Creatures lurk around in fear,
Watching the land so carefully.
Fish swimming with grace,
Under a life-filled endless sea.

Humans live within this world,
Struggling to make ends meet.
Broken pieces tossed around,
Sweating to build once more in the
fiery heat.

Standing there with emotions,
That I can't quite understand.
A sad feeling in my gut,
What happened to their land?
My friend has shown me beauty,

But also a world of destruction.
Not every person struggles here,
Only the ones with no instruction.

Massive skyscrapers reach to the sky,
Tearing apart the nature that lived there first.
Those builders care only about expansion,
For greed is their only thirst.

Many different things to see,
That only with my own eyes I can believe.
Big cities can thrive,
Leaving my villagers to grieve.

Learning every person has their own story,
Every creature and human in the world.
Each and every has a life that matters,
Even the flowers who cannot say a word.

Wow! Should I be a ninja poet who talks to
turtles someday?! Hmmm.

Day 10

I have taken in so much valuable information lately. I took a journey with my friend last night to see more of what he wanted to show me. Tonight, we are meeting up because during the day today, River is going to listen in to conversations of the poor villagers. I should have a better outlook on things when I get there. Also, I need to see if the iron hoe has been used to create that garden! Hold on tight, portal. Here we come!

Diary, I did not have time to write while in the other world. I'm here now, back at home. Something wasn't right as soon as I arrived through the portal. I could feel it. I could sense it. I was creeping closer to the tall tree on the rolling hill before me. At the meeting spot, River was nowhere to be found! Where was he? What's going on? I didn't feel good at all! Even the wind wasn't howling. Everything around me looked different and the feeling I had was making me nervous! My throat got choked up, and I had chills running all throughout my body.

Nope. That wasn't choking. My lunch came out of my mouth, and I threw up on the ground. Ew, gross!! I did not want to see that, so I walked away, hoping nobody else saw that! Being nervous can really do something crazy to a body. Yikes! Still, where was River? I was so worried! Pushing that feeling aside for a moment, I went to go check on the iron hoe.

I couldn't seem to stop thinking about my friend. Even though I was bothered by this, I was glad to see a garden in the works! I wonder if this villager is curious about these gifts. Afterall, it isn't his birthday. Well, I'm guessing it isn't. Then the craziest thing happened! A fluffy creature with long ears and huge, menacing buck teeth hopped toward me! All I could think of in that terrifying moment was to hiss! Hiss! Hiss! Hiss! Shaking my trembling body, I released my vibrant purple floaties to swirl around me! Back away! Back away, you rabbit! Ninja moves! I tried some ninja moves so maybe he wouldn't get close to me! I told him to stop hopping like that! I knew who he was! River has told me that they are harmless, but I didn't trust his hopping abilities and those tall weird-looking ears! Back away! Hiss!

The rabbit was gone. I think I scared him. When you go through scary rabbit situations, you must write about it in your diary! My adventures must be told! Oh River, where are you? I could hear the howling wind. It's hard to distinguish between the wind howl and the howl of my fearless friend. As I looked around to the left and the right, the howling became louder. I stood frozen like a statue.

The eerie noise was getting close to me. The noise wa
moving! There were a lot of howling voices. Was it a pacl
of wolves? If it was, there were way too many wolves fo
my liking. I knew that I had to get back home and hopefull
my companion would be okay and meet me at our spo
tomorrow. Hopefully!

Day 11

I'm trembling. I can't stop shaking. Oh diary, I did not have a good start to my night here in the world beyond. I'm here, in the villagers' world. I am so sorry that it took me this long to write in you. Being safe is all that I should be focused on. I think I'm safe. The moment that I arrived through the portal, was also the very moment I had to run for my life. In the distance, I can hear them. There are echoes of angry voices swirling around through the air. I have to explain what happened and I believe I'm safe enough right now to do so.

Here is how it started. Taking a cautious step forward out of the portal, normally that's the time I recover from my dizziness. There was no time for that. Three villagers were standing close to the entrance as if they were patiently waiting for me. All three humans were tightly gripping their golden swords. Defending myself would have been easy when all they had were weak, gold swords. I learned all about different weapons from the others at home.

But, I couldn't. I mean, I wouldn't. I just wouldn't want to harm them at all! That's not me! They have every right to be nervous about seeing me, I am an enderman. Oh, how I wish the world beyond could see the good I have within. Unfortunately, that moment was not the time for me to try to explain why I was there, and I couldn't risk what might happen if they stared into my glowing eyes.

Without any hesitation, I teleported. Then, I ran and I ran some more. Speeding through forests of trees, buzzing past small animals, I kept going. Dodging low hanging branches, I was as swift as a flying bat and as nimble as a ninja. I knew that the villagers were still out there looking to defeat me. Suddenly, the sky started to rumble. I knew what it was. The other endermen warned me about this! It was churning from above, getting ready to release water drops from the clouds. I had to find shelter from the rain. That's when I discovered the dark cave I am sitting in right now.

The trembling, it won't go away. I am still trembling. Even though I really pulled off some ninja moves tonight, I'm not happy about what I just went through. The small opening to the world beyond is the only entrance and exit to this cave. Rain. I see the tiny water teardrops splashing onto the ground. Each raindrop lands so violently. I've never seen rain. I know I should fear it but since this cave is deep underground, I know I'll be okay. I have to be okay!

The sound it makes is rather peaceful. Plop. Dink. Splash. Nature sure is a funny thing. Suddenly feeling extremely relaxed, I imagine myself back in my home world where I always feel safe. I don't know where I am. I ran fast as lightning. I could be anywhere. River has shown me only a little of this land. He said it's way bigger than I could imagine. I'm stuck here. It's going to be a long night.

Villagers are lucky. They can stand in the dripping rain falling from the sky with no worries at all. Even the thought of dancing in the rain makes me jealous. I've got some good moves, not to pat myself on the back or anything. I do love dancing. Obviously, I never show off my moves for the other endermen. They never bust a move. I'm different. Wishing I could shuffle around at this water party, I hear a faint noise, almost like a whisper in the wind.

The villagers are still out there. I only hope they do no find me trembling in my dirt-filled home for the night Enchanting noises from the rainstorm are starting to calm my fear of being caught. Time to try to get some much-needed rest.

Day 12

It's a new night. I must have slept through an entire day, but I feel like I just fell asleep. Glancing towards the cave opening, I see that the sky is still dark. I took a rest, but sadly, the rain did not. Water is still dripping from the sky, but it's more of a sprinkle now, almost as if a giant is using a watering can to feed the flowers. Good. I'm glad the flowers are getting a drink so that they can survive, but I'm ready for it to stop storming so I can find my way home.

Silence is eerie. All that I can hear now is the slow drip of water drops and some sort of echo coming from deep within the cave. It's a shuffling kind of sound. I think that's what woke me up to begin with. Either that or knowing that I'm stuck in an unknown part of this world. Telling myself that I am Enderman keeps my trembling body at ease somewhat. I am brave now. If I can deliver goodies to villagers who believe I'm a scary monster and become friends with a wolf, I can do anything.

I see dark figures moving along the sides of my shelter. I see several red glowing lights right where the shadows are creeping. They seem to be peeking at me from the shadows. Shuffle. Shuffle. That's the only sound coming from this mysterious creature. I can squint my eyes to see more clearly. With a better view, I know what he is. This is a cave spider and I mean him no harm, but I will defend myself if I must. He looks at me as if he means me no harm as well. It's like I can connect with his thoughts. I just feel it. He is not coming any closer. Actually, he just went further into the darkness.

The plopping sound of the rain is slowing down. Oh no. The sun is coming up! I have never been here during the day. Wow! Over that faraway hill, I can see the horizon changing to light pink and purple, completely erasing the dark colors of a moment earlier. It's breathtaking! It's something so simple, something everyone can share, and yet, it's something humans take for granted. Maybe if they stopped their busy lives for just a moment, they could see the beauty right before them.

The pink and purple sky has a bright yellowish ball rising from the hill. It looks like it's floating straight up from the green hilltop. Incredible! As soon as the sun lifted high above the hill, the rain vanished with the darkness. Whoa! I'll never forget this moment. I am so glad I have you here with me so that I can write down and remember every detail.

What now? I'm so glad I saw that. For a moment, I forgot all about my troubles and knew nothing but the sunrise. Time to get back to reality. I mean, I have been in reality the whole time. I'm in a cave with a red-eyed spider for goodness' sake! Honestly though, let's get to it! It's daytime. I have a feeling that this will be my biggest mission yet. Where exactly am

I and how on earth can I avoid all living creatures?! It's time to put you back in my pack. I need to figure out where I am

I'm home now! Something always happens on my adventures This is how the rest of the day went for me. That cave was like a turtle shell, and I extended my block-shaped head out to peek at the brightly lit world. I was overwhelmed. "Okay take a breath," I told myself. "Relax. It's okay! I'm used to the darkness, but that doesn't mean I should fear the light." Feeling comforted with that thought, I was now able to think straight. The colors! The sounds! The life! It was all so much to take in.

Suddenly, I let out an annoying little screech! "AHHHHH! That was not funny at all! How dare you, River!!" Okay, okay, time to explain. The very moment I was surrounded by overwhelming noises and bright colors, River peeked his puppy head right into the cave opening! Why was he laughing? My screech did sound a little odd. Alright, thinking about that has me chuckling right now, just as my friend did. I can't be mad at him for spooking me. After all, I was worried sick about him and I'm glad to see he's okay.

I found out that River has superpowers just like I do! He has a crazy sense of smell. Wait a minute here… Is he telling me that I smell? What do I smell like?! Hmm… hopefully it's the scent of fresh flowers and not an odor rotting meat would give off! He sniffed around the land to follow my scent. The wind, with my scent attached, led him to the cave! I wish I had that superpower!

Working together we made a plan to get me back to the portal. River knows his world like the back of his paw! We were headed towards a group of gray, staggered mountains. I really needed to focus. It's very hard to do when everything is so bright. It hardly seems real.

River was my bodyguard today. With his fierce, white fangs, even a scary rabbit wouldn't try to take me down! Take that, you silly rabbit! There weren't any villagers in sight, and I knew why. An enormous cloud of smoke was coming from behind the distant mountains. It floated up higher, rising gracefully. River explained to me that the amount of smoke we saw looked like it was coming from a big fire. We still had a long way to go before we'd be able to see where it was coming from.

As we passed through a jungle, I heard a rustling in the leaves. I hid behind a tree where the bark was peeling away from the trunk. I stayed there until River scared away an ocelot. Dog versus cat! That was interesting! I was not afraid of the ocelot, but I was afraid of harming him. River took care of it so that I don't have to live with that feeling! He really is a good friend! The big cat just wanted to play, but we needed him to get away. Ah, I did it again! Enderman The Ninja Poet!! Hehe!

Anyways, turns out the village that I have been on a mission to help, sits right behind the massive mountains up ahead. When we climbed over the mountain, I saw that the smoke was coming from the village! All I could hear was screaming! They needed help and I couldn't help with this problem. All I kept thinking was "What can I do?" River and I ran toward the village. Red and orange flames were taking over multiple homes!! It was the scariest thing I have ever seen! Even more scary than a rabbit hopping towards me!! River told me to stay away from the village, but I wanted to help so bad. I guess sometimes I need to realize that I can't do everything. I knew I shouldn't risk my life, but I had to know that the villagers would be okay.

It was a horrible scene to watch. Screaming, running, carrying buckets of water everywhere, the villagers were working together to fix the problem. Their houses were more ruined than before. With tears in my eyes, I turned and walked away. I found the portal and I'm back at home now. I hope I don't have a nightmare about fire, rabbits, red eyed spiders, and rain drops tonight!

Day 13

It was hard to get to sleep last night with everything on my mind. Today, I will look around my world to see what I can bring to the villagers. They need supplies. Especially after the blazing heat that demolished more of their homes! Let me see what I can find!

Okay, so I now have cobblestone, a diamond pickaxe, carrots, milk, cookies, terracotta, and dirt. The cobblestone, terracotta, and dirt should not be flammable. Hopefully, all these goodies will fit into my pack. Okay, everything fits! I placed the carrots, milk, and cookies into a chest and the blocks and pickaxe are safe in my pack! Taking a brief look around, I'm in the clear to jump into my favorite ride!

Back at home! It's time to share details of tonight's journey. I saw River waiting patiently by our meeting tree. I found out from him that the reason he didn't show up the other night was because he had to fight a battle with his pack. River is tough. Tougher than a ninja, in my opinion.

He had the courage to scare away zombies that surrounded his family. Sometimes, life doesn't go as expected. I like learning from all situations. If something bad happens, all you can do is try to fix it! Even if it's too late to fix the problem, I've learned that it's okay to fail. Sometimes, the best thing you can do with a bad time, is learn from it. That way, hopefully, you know how to stop other bad things from happening in the future. Life can be tough, but I think I'm slowly figuring it out!

River has told me about the conversations the villagers had amongst themselves when I went back home last night. They are devastated. Something keeps taking items from them and they barely have anything left to survive. So many people of that town were heard sobbing and River got the immediate feeling that they just gave up. We have to fix this!

After our short conversation, we made it closer to the town. All I could smell was burnt wood and I saw ashes scattered all around. It was sad. I'd much rather enjoy the scent of thriving flowers. The house in the far-right corner had been greatly damaged by the fire. That's where I placed the cobblestone, dirt, and terracotta..

River had the chest of food and I told him that he can pick a lucky villager to give it to. He is always helpful! Maybe we should invent a team name for us. How about "The Living Lunatics"? No, "The Helpful Ham Sandwiches"? No, maybe "The Ninja Nutshells"? I got it! We are the "The Brave Brothers"! BB! That's perfect!

Day 14

I already made my trip to the other world today. Looking at the devastation I saw the previous night, it was very hard for me to remember the glorious beauty I saw during the daylight hours. I was there once again, wondering what the night will bring, since life can be mysterious. I am a ninja enderman! Being sneaky is one of my fantastic abilities. I do not like to use my powers for evil! I know what I'm capable of, but I use all my energy only for good! I'm glad I was able to help the villagers.

I met up with River and we were taking a lovely stroll down the hillside towards the village. We got there, and my, oh my,the villagers work fast! The cobblestone and terracotta were already being used as a replacement for the homes that were tragically burnt down. Awesome!

The chest of food was also inside the home where River left it. That's also good! Who would've thought that survival is such hard work?! I now look at these villagers in a whole new way. Of course, they attack us when we are spotted.

That's part of their survival. They know that many endermen have cruel intentions. I hope that someday they can appreciate my odd behavior. I probably wouldn't even have time to explain who I am before they finish me off for good.

I saw someone! River and I were taking cover behind a house that had all the lights off. The moon was being blocked by the clouds, so natural light was hard to come by. Then, oh no!! I saw one of my own. What was he doing?! I couldn't let him take that cobblestone I just gifted! River wanted to try to scare him away, but that's too dangerous for him. I made a move. My identity needed to be hidden.

I grabbed a pumpkin that was on the ground and placed it onto my block head. Woohoo! I magically transformed into a jack-o-lantern ninja!! It was time to act spooky and scare away that enderman! . I ran at him with my incredible speed, pumpkin-head and all! The snort laugh is coming because I keep thinking about what I must look like to the other enderman. Just imagine it! Imagine a long-legged, dark figure coming at you with a pumpkin as a head. Yeah, he won't be able to sleep tonight! Hehe!

Day 15

Taking some time to reflect on my adventures so far, I never really realized how many adventures I could have by just trying to be helpful. I've learned a lot! Even through the scariest of times, I must be brave.

Tonight, in the world beyond my own, I met up with River and we already had a problem! You never know what life can throw at you. Every night brings new possibilities and new obstacles to overcome.

River told me that the villagers were being attacked. We had to hurry. Standing at a good distance, I witnessed something I had never seen before. These creatures were as green as a freshly picked apple! They were walking around the village with their arms reaching out in front of them! Time to attack some zombies, I told myself. I am quick, and with all of the commotion, I doubted that I would even be noticed by the villagers.

It was awesome! Most of the people went back into their homes while the zombie army was in full force all around them. The diamond pickaxe that I brought to the villagers was lying by a fountain. Making sure that I didn't get splashed, I picked up the pickaxe and ran at full speed towards the zombies! Yes, I know I said that I don't want to harm any creature, but this was a necessity. River was very impressed with my ability to fight off evil! Thank goodness I have been taught to fight by the other endermen.

After defeating those green minions, I rushed back home so that the villagers would not spot me. That was exhausting but thrilling at the same time. River will report to me tomorrow night under our tree.

Day 16

It's been sixteen days since I started writing about my adventures in a new world. Even though I have been stuck in tough situations, I have risen above them and fought through them every single time. I'm proud of myself! Now, I need to find weapons for the people of the town. I found a shield, crossbow, bow, and arrows. This will do for now.

Sneaking to the portal, I was caught. I'm now sitting down at my happy spot in my world. I am upset about what just happened. There's no way I can go to the other world tonight. River is going to be worried. If only I had a way to reach him so that he could know I'm not coming. This is just awful!

Right when I was getting ready to jump in the swirling portal, one of my own crept up behind me and said, "What are you doing, young one?" Because I am so different from them, lying is hard for me to do. I stood there holding my breath, and, thinking quickly, I said, "I'm ready to explore a new place." It was the next question that I wasn't ready for. The other enderman then asked, "Why do you need weapons when your body is a weapon by itself?" with a little hesitation, I replied, "Um… I feel safer having other options."

He stood there in complete silence and just glared at me for a moment. I quickly ended the encounter by telling him that I may need some more time before I'm comfortable going out into other worlds by myself. I also thanked him for reminding me of what my lanky body is capable of. Coming up with a new plan sounds like a great idea right now. Let's think here. Okay, I got it! I'm going to stay in the other world for the next couple of days! I lived through the brightness of the day once before! I can do it again!

Day 17

All packed up! I have the weapons that I want to bring to the villagers. I hope that River isn't too worried about what happened last night. He will probably be excited when I inform him that I will be staying for a few days. The other endermen don't really notice anyone missing from the group. Honestly, they don't seem to care about much at all. Here I go!

As soon as I made it, I saw my fluffy friend! I was right. River was worried but we are okay now because we are back on track with being secret ninja helpers! Team BB at it once again! My teammate told me that he spied on the villagers today. They were speaking of the zombie attack and how they have no idea where the green and creepy creatures went. That's okay friends! I took care of that with my tiny muscles and a diamond pickaxe!

We started to walk towards the village and heard many mysterious sounds creeping through the air. River has taught me a lot about this unknown world. My favorite thing that he has shared with me was something he told me the day he found me in the cave. If you look high above you, in the darkness of the night, the stars and moon are always at the same spot. This is how I can find my way if I ever become lost. Also, during the bright day, if the shining sun isn't hiding behind clouds, its location in the sky will tell me what time it is. Learning and expanding my knowledge makes me feel even more powerful than I ever have.

The shield has been placed at one home's doorstep, the crossbow is hanging out by another, and the bow and arrows are now resting at a different home. Mission complete. An enderman better not touch those items or I'll be a jack-o-lantern chasing them for some Halloween candy! River and I moved away from the town, taking in every sound we heard from all directions. Buzz, swoosh, the wind encircling us as we swiftly stroll further away from the houses. We needed to set up camp. I'm here to stay for a couple of days!

Day 18

Let's start this day off with a poem, brought to you by a fearless enderman!

I found a shelter,
Cold and dark like my home.
They call this a dungeon,
Standing tall in this biome.

Creeping creatures live within,
Placing shadows on the wall.
It's no scarier than my world,
But it is rather tall.

My friend went home,
To be with his pack tonight.
He has to be there,
In case he needs to fight.

So, here I am using this dungeon as my temporary home. It's cozy, as long as nothing comes around to spook me! The sun will be rising soon and a fun-filled day it will bring. Ha! I can only hope! That sunrise! I remember it so well! Taking a look around, lively characters are everywhere. Bumblebees seem to be on their own adventure, flying gracefully through the air, buzzing wings fluttering fast. River told me that the sound is coming from how fast their wings move.

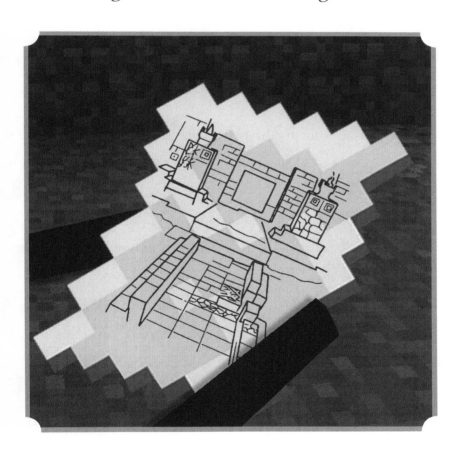

I went to the village. I was supposed to meet River there. I had to go through a small forest of magnificent trees to reach my destination. A lot of noise happens during the day. Silence is not an option during bright hours here. I wanted to meet my buddy at the village because I wanted to find courage to reach the houses all by myself. I can't always rely on my furry and fanged friend!

When approaching the village, I thought that I had made a wrong turn. Gazing up at the blinding sun, I believe I was headed west like I should be. Glancing over the grassy hills, there was nothing there. All I could see was broken down rubble! This couldn't be! Oh no! Please tell me that this can't be! I didn't see a single person in sight! What was that all over the land's surface? Broken pieces from homes, scattered, half-eaten fruit and vegetables, arrows split in half, and farm animals carelessly walking around looking very confused. I was confused too. It can't be the village. Oh, but it was! Sitting there among the destruction was the statue that one of my own tried to steal! Everything was gone! Feeling terrified of whatever could have done this, I teleported back to the dungeon.

River has no idea where I am. I hope he will think of coming to the dungeon. I'm sending him secret ninja brainwaves to tell him where I am. What am I talking about? My brain can't be that powerful to talk to another brain without speaking! Or can it? There is way too much on my mind. I must rest.

Day 19

I slept. I slept for so long. Sometimes, I think that when you feel that tired, your body is trying to tell you that it needs rest. Even though I woke feeling refreshed, I still had nightmares about what might have happened in the village. There were so many possibilities. Maybe the Ender Dragon flew above the town spitting blazing fire at everything in his sight. I had another dream where thousands of brown, hopping rabbits took control and tore up the place. Bad rabbits!!! I also dreamt that all the endermen from my world showed up in suits of armor, marching to go to battle with the town. With all the tossing and turning, I probably didn't rest as much as my body needed last night.

River is here now, and the day has begun. He saw exactly what I saw last night. No, not the Ender Dragon, rabbits, or endermen ready for battle! He saw everything in the village destroyed making the land flat with no houses to be seen. Something doesn't seem right. The thoughts of what could have happened to those innocent people is upsetting. Deep in thought, I'm quiet. I'm definitely not my usual, outgoing self today!

We traveled back toward the destroyed town in a sad daze without talking much. Surrounded by nature that is still thriving, the village was left to pieces, wishing it had the chance to thrive. There were people, but not many, standing as if frozen in ice. These people worked hard to survive and now they have to start all over building their homes from nothing. Will they even rebuild? Oh, they looked very sad. How could I possibly help?

Suddenly, while walking through the forest to get to the town, I spotted something that looked weird to me. Something was buried beneath a grassy area!! AAAAHHHH!!!! Whoa! Wow! I just found some sort of a trap door in the ground! There is a long ladder going further down into the ground. The ladder looks like it never stops! What is this?! River is staying above ground to be my lookout partner in case anything comes near where we are. Hold on diary, I'm taking you with me!

I just reached the end of the ladder. There doesn't seem to be any strange creature down here. I should be okay to write down what I see. There are hallways lined with flames on top of sticks to light the way. Oh, please flames, do not start a fire as big as the one that I saw taking over the village! I'm beyond scared as I explore this strange place! I'm on edge. I see a room extending off the hallway about ten blocks in front of me. Slowly, I'm moving my head into the room to get a better view. There are multiple chests in there. One of them is slightly open and I can see the stem of an apple poking out. Gardening tools, various weapons, and cooked meat are scattered around. What is this place? I want to explore more of this underground whatever it is! I'll be right back. I have to yell up to River to tell him I'm fine and still looking around.

Day 20

Holding you in my shaking hands, I hope my handwriting is okay! I'm so scared! While exploring the underground bunker, I saw a shadow on the back wall. The shadow was getting bigger! The smokey shadow got very big!! The shadow was moving to the ground and off the wall. Who was that? I saw something coming around the corner. The figure was standing there and it was looking in my direction. It looked like a human form, but it wasn't a villager. I have to write this all down for evidence!!

This creature was wearing a purple top, had a long nose pointing away from its head, and a black funny looking thing on top of its head. The nose had bumps on it. Like little bubbles! I didn't like that nose. I didn't like that nose one bit! The creature was not talking to me. It stood there motionless, just as I was. I didn't even have time to try to lock eyes with the bumpy nosed creature. I wanted to, so that I can pull off my attack mode with ease. I had a strange feeling that it wasn't friendly.

I yelled for River and then everything went black, even darker than my world.

Right now, I'm in a place where I feel stuck. Metal poles are surrounding me, and I can barely move! This place is scary! This place is not comforting at all. I want to go home! Thankfully, I have you here with me. I don't know where I am or how long I've been here. What happened? Was this all a dream? Nope, I just pinched myself and I'm still here. This is reality?!? It can't be.

Oh, the noise I'm hearing sounds like pure pain! Every direction I look, I see red, and the heat in this place is unbearable! I'm stuck in a cage while these white blobs are floating up towards the ceiling. Or is that the sky? I'm so confused. The screaming sound coming from these creatures is the spookiest noise I've ever heard!! They spit out balls of fire like the Ender Dragon! I'm not moving from this cage, even if I could. Dark, brick-red blocks are jumping! A fiery liquid on the ground looks like a discolored stream of sparkling water. This stream is not as beautiful as the one in the other world. It's so hot here!

Closing my glowing eyes for a second or two, I daydream of the green, rolling hills, the staggered mountains, sunrises, buzzing bees, and my dear friend who must be worried sick! I'd much rather be surrounded by pesky rabbits even though rabbits freak me out! Uh oh!!!! In the corner of my eye, once my daydream vanished into thin air, I can see a figure. It's hard to write and be so scared at the same time. It's a villager. We just locked eyes!

THE END(erman)

Made in the USA
Las Vegas, NV
07 November 2023

80425835R00049